Greeks Bearing Gifts

Ilene T. Goldman

Book Layout & Design ©2017 - BookDesignTemplates.com
Cover Design -Fantasy & Coffee Design

Greeks Bearing Gifts/ Ilene T. Goldman. -- 1st ed.
ISBN 979-8-9865962-1-1

Beware of Greeks bearing gifts.

–Proverb

1.

J.D. punched the numbers again. Could that be right? He flipped over an envelope—his electric bill, with a bright red PAST DUE stamp on the front—and did the calculations by hand: his paycheck plus the last of his savings, carry the one just like Miss Domenico taught him.

Was that right? He did it again.

He turned to the little white mouse that had crawled out on the counter. "Well how about that?"

He could actually pay rent this month.

The mouse scurried away, to whatever little cubby he and his friends had found behind the cabinets.

Okay, so not J.D's *whole* rent. But a nice chunk. More than he'd been able to pay in months. Enough to get the landlord off his case for a couple of weeks. Or, better yet, pay the landlord a little less and knock a bit off the overdue gas bill. It wouldn't do any good to have the gas shut off just as Mother Nature was getting her chill on.

J.D. leaned back, the chair squeaking under his weight. He let out a long, heavy breath.

Just as relief reached his core, his phone rang. His wicked witch ringtone, no less. He could let it go to voicemail, but, no, that would be worse.

He pressed the green button. "Elaine."

"Are you going to make me ask again?"

"Now what did I do?"

"You know damn well it's what you *didn't* do. Again. For chrissakes, J.D., Nick is your child, too. A few hundred dollars—"

"We've been through this, Elaine. Many times. Two of them in court."

"A few hundred a month in child support is not asking much. Especially since—"

"You didn't ask for alimony." J.D. rolled his eyes. "Yeah, I know. And if I could make my payments, I would. In case you've forgotten, I've been out of work. For a while. Money's not exactly rolling in. That's why the court—"

"I know for a fact that you got paid yesterday." Her tone plunged a knife into J.D.'s spine.

J.D. fingered the paycheck that he had, in fact, received the day before. Clearly, Elaine's facts were limited. The paycheck amounted to all of $83 after taxes, the proceeds from the one day of temp work he'd had in the last two weeks, only the second day of work he'd had in three months.

Elaine liked to bat around the word *lazy*, even before the divorce, but J.D.'s lack of work lately was not from lack of effort. Since the factory shut down, the temp agency had more workers than openings. They did their best to rotate men through the jobs. It was never enough. But try telling her that.

"Elaine, do you know how much that check was? It wasn't even big enough for the court to garnish."

She muttered something, but J.D. couldn't quite make it out.

"Look, I'm no deadbeat. I don't have the money, but I do have time. More than I know what to do with. The court said I could pay in hours. Let me do that. I'll change the oil in your car. I'll paint your living room. Give something to do, and I'll do it."

"I can't pay my bills with your time, J.D." Then she twisted the knife. "If you truly loved your son, you'd find the cash."

The click of her hanging up echoed in J.D.'s ear. He stared at the phone and blinked. Find a way? What did she want him to do? Rob a bank? Sell an organ? Off himself?

His gaze wandered to the window and the gray clouds that padded the sky. He'd considered that last option, offing himself, more than once. As his savings account dwindled over the last few months, the thought occurred with greater frequency. But J.D. never had been a man of action, so that's all it ever stayed—a thought.

Besides, it's not like his Ms. Real Estate Broker of the Year ex-wife actually needed his money. She was doing fine without him. She just wanted to bleed him dry. It was her favorite sport.

He did miss Nick. It was a perennial hollow ache in his gut. When was the last time they spent any real time together? How much did he really know about Nick's day to day life? J.D. tried to list Nick's friends. He came up with one, maybe two names. Surely Nick had more pals than that. What kind of father didn't know the names of his kid's friends?

No. J.D. slammed his hand on the table. That was Elaine talking, her voice an insidious virus planted in his brain. She was not going to win. No way he was going to let her take Nick away from him. No way.

Elaine wielded their son like a weapon, dangled him like a carrot on a stick. All J.D. had to do was pay. Extortion, that's what it was. Blackmail. If he could afford a lawyer, he'd fight her on it. But lawyers—like everything else—cost money.

J.D. pushed the phone away and Elaine out of his thoughts. He looked at his back-of-the-envelope calculations again, trying to recapture some of the good mood they'd created. But all he could think about was Nick.

To clear his head, J.D. threw on some sweats and went for a walk—faster when Elaine or money skulked in his head, slower when he managed to push those thoughts away. He arrived back home shiny with sweat, his worry knots slightly looser.

J.D. stepped out of the shower to the sound of his phone, this time playing his son's ringtone, the opening riff from Peter Gabriel's "Solsbury Hill." *Son of a gun.* He accepted the call before the tone could repeat. "Hey, kid."

"Hey, Dad."

J.D. checked the clock. "Aren't you in school? Shouldn't you be in class?"

"Yeah, but it's flex time. I didn't want to call from home. Mom doesn't want me talking to you."

J.D. gave silent thanks for the rebelliousness of teenagers. "Yeah, I know. I owe her some money, and—"

Nick sighed, sounding more like a 70-year-old man than a 17-year-old boy. "You're still my dad."

"That I am, but be careful. I don't want you to get in trouble with your mother. I don't want you to get in trouble with your teachers, either. Are you sure it's okay for you to be calling me now?"

"Yeah, Dad, it's fine."

"As long as you're sure—"

"I am."

"All right. So what's going on? School going okay?" J.D. traced the figures on the envelope with his finger.

"Yeah, school's fine."

"You got your hockey schedule yet?"

"Not yet. We don't even get on the ice until next month."

"I thought practices had started already?"

"They did, but it's mostly conditioning."

"Strong legs, kid. Strong legs." J.D. had no idea what that meant, but everyone that Nick ever played for used that mantra.

Nick chuckled. "Yeah, that's what coach keeps saying too."

"Yeah, well, don't forget to send me the schedule when you get it. I wouldn't be doing my job as your father if I didn't embarrass you at your games now and again."

J.D. could hear Nick's smile. "Yeah, Dad, I know."

An awkward silence fell between them. When had J.D. lost the ability to talk to his son? They used to jabber for hours—about the Tigers line-up, the Pistons' playoff chances, Nick's little-boy dreams of being a Red Wings defenseman, an astronaut, or a firefighter, the color of the sky, the fish in the lake, a million little things that were of no importance at all, until now when they seemed to have lost the words for them.

"Dad?"

"Yeah."

"Um, I know Mom's pestering you for money but—"

J.D. closed his eyes and pinched his nose. "What do you need?"

"New gear. Mom's already paid all the school fees."

He took a slow, deep breath. "How much?"

"About $500. Maybe a little more."

Another deep breath. "Okay, break it down for me."

Nick did. Skates, pads, guards, gloves—all told came to $565.

"Okay. I'm not making any promises, but I'll see what I can do. I'll call you back."

"Thanks, Dad. It's better if you just text, though. In case Mom's around."

"Good call."

J.D. put the phone on the table and his head in his hands. He wallowed for a few minutes before pulling the calculator, envelope, and pencil back in front of him. Under his calculations, he listed what Nick had told him. At $250, the skates were the most expensive item.

He punched the numbers into his calculator. He could swing the skates. It would just mean a smaller chunk for his landlord. And no payment on his electric bill.

He stared at the numbers, his heart and belly hollow. He'd let Nick down so much already. Maybe he could manage more than just the skates.

More numbers crunched. Then even more. Until he had all $565 in his calculations.

He texted Nick. *I got you. Full amount. You want to stop by for the check?*

So much for his rent. Or heat. Or even eating. Eighteen months of unemployment, gone. A lifetime of savings, run out. Paycheck spent before he ever got it. How the hell did he end up here? He threw the calculator against the wall. It clattered to the floor and splintered on the worn linoleum. The battery popped out and rolled a few inches across the floor.

Meanwhile, the sun broke through the clouds, sending its rays through the window like a spotlight on the pieces of calculator. J.D. stared at the tableau. There was a metaphor in there somewhere, he was sure, but he'd be damned if he could figure out what it was.

He let the pieces lie.

2.

The next morning, J.D. stood in his kitchenette, coffee in hand, the wheels in his head turning. He was giving his last pennies to Nick, but he still had to eat. It wouldn't hurt to throw a few bucks his landlord's direction, either. Or the gas company, for that matter. He reached over and turned down the thermostat.

A call to the temp agency had led nowhere. The local want ads were the same ol' sparse collection of false promises—sales jobs, mostly. But who would he sell to in a town that had more ghosts than people?

He surveyed what remained of his kingdom, all 698 square feet of it. The furnishings were sparse, but he could probably sell off a few.

The kitchen table and chairs could go. He ate most of his meals in his armchair. The laptop could go. It wasn't much use without the internet, and he'd given up that subscription six months ago. He could do without the microwave too. How much could all that fetch?

He made up some numbers, with no idea if they were low-balls or overestimates. The exercise did nothing to calm the flutters of his anxiety.

A knock on the door goosed him.

"Yo, J.D. It's Kurt." Another insistent knock. "You there?"

So much for his luck turning around. His landlord at the door once again proved the enduring theme of his life: if it weren't for bad luck, he'd have no luck at all.

J.D. threw a silent curse and swung open the door. "Hey, Kurt."

"J.D." Kurt walked in as if he owned the place, which technically he did. He was dressed in his usual uniform: t-shirt, dirty jeans, scuffed-up tennis shoes. His hair probably started out combed this morning, but now stood every which way—a sure sign that he'd been fixing something at one of his properties. The dark stains on his knuckles confirmed it.

"Can I get you something?" J.D. asked. "I don't have much, but I could manage a glass of water."

Kurt leaned back against the counter and crossed his arms and his ankles. "Rent would be nice. Could you manage that?"

"Get straight to the point, why dontcha?"

J.D.'s mouse friend peered out and took a few tentative steps onto the counter. Its movement caught Kurt's attention.

"You want me to take care of that?" Kurt asked. "I got some traps and poison out in my car."

"Nah. Let him be. He's no trouble."

Kurt nodded toward the mouse. "Except they never travel alone. Where there's one, there's a hundred."

"It's fine."

Kurt bent down and opened the under-sink cabinet. He gestured at the droppings scattered around the garbage can. "They carry that hantavirus, too, you know."

"I know. Let's just say we've come to an agreement. And yes, I will clean that up."

Kurt dropped into a squat. "Look, I'm not trying to be a hardass. But I am your landlord, and you do owe me rent."

"You are, and I do." J.D. took a deep breath. "But I don't have it yet. Give me a couple of days, and I'll get you something."

Kurt shook his head.

"You know I'm good for it," J.D. said. "I know I haven't paid in full in a while, but I've given you what I can every month. This month isn't any different."

Kurt stared at J.D. It wasn't a mean or disbelieving look, but one of assessment, like he was trying to decide something. Then he broke contact and pushed himself upright. "Here's the thing. The bank is coming after me, dropping words like *delinquent* and *foreclosure* and *repossession*. I need to make things right with them, but to do that, I need you to make things right with me."

J.D. bit his tongue. It wasn't his fault that Kurt was overextended. It wasn't his fault that Kurt was property rich and cash poor. It wasn't his job to solve Kurt's problem. Kurt was the one who'd bought up the houses on the block, back when the housing bubble burst. He was the one who saw the properties as wise investments and easy money, even though the town was already dying around them.

"How many apartments you got these days?" J.D. asked.

"Ten."

"How many are occupied?"

"Four. Five, if you count the one I live in."

"So you got four tenants." J.D. crossed his arms. "Why are you putting it on my shoulders to put you in the black?"

"It's not just on your shoulders." Kurt knocked on the kitchen table. "You're like a leg of this table. The table needs all four of its legs to stand, and I need all four of my tenants to pay their rent."

"And if I can't pay in full? Are you gonna evict me?"

"I don't want it to come to that."

"But it could come to that."

Kurt nodded. "Yes, it could."

"Then what? You have three tenants and six vacant units, and you still won't be able to pay the bank. In fact, it will be even harder because your table will have only three legs."

"Not if I—"

"Not if you find another tenant to take this place? Like you've found new tenants for all your other vacant units? Good luck with that." J.D. stepped closer to Kurt, but not close enough to be antagonistic. "I'm the best bet you've got, and we both know it."

J.D. held out his hand. "Just give me a couple more days. I swear I'll get you as much as I can."

Kurt grimaced but accepted the handshake. "You better."

The door hadn't clicked shut behind Kurt when J.D.'s phone rang. *Damn it.* Couldn't he at least take a breath?

MIDWEST COLLECT, his Caller ID announced in big capital letters.

J.D. dismissed the call.

Minutes later, as J.D. was settling into his armchair, it rang again. CAPITAL MGMT.

He dismissed that call too.

Damn collection agencies. They could keep calling all they wanted, but that wasn't going to put the money they demanded into his pockets. Vultures, that's what they were, stalking the weak. Well, they could pry his last pennies from his cold, dead hands.

His eyes landed on the pile of bills on his counter. Assuming he had any pennies left by then.

A knock on the door stopped him cold. Kurt again? Another collection agent? Someone else who wanted to pick his pocket? J.D. froze, not even daring to breathe.

Another knock. "Dad? You home?"

Nick. J.D. exhaled, pushing down his anger, making room for a little spark of cheer. Any day he got to see his son—even if it was only for a few minutes—was, by definition, a good day.

"Hey, kid." J.D. greeted his son with a handshake. His kid wasn't a kid anymore. Legally, still a minor, yes, but more confident, more self-sufficient, more settled than any child. Tall, lean, good looking—what J.D.'s parents would have called a ladykiller. Definitely not something the boy got from J.D.'s side of the family, if the pudge J.D. saw in the mirror every morning was any indication.

Nick followed his dad into the apartment, dropping his backpack on the kitchen table with a thud. He fished in one of the pockets. "Before I forget . . ."

He dug a bit more and pulled out a sheet of paper with a bright blue and yellow border. Good ol' Darian High School colors. "Here's my game schedule."

"Thanks." J.D. grabbed the paper and pinned it to the front of his refrigerator with a dirty Pizza Time magnet. Then he slid an envelope from under the Jade House Chinese magnet. "And this is for you."

"Thanks, Dad. I really appreciate it." The envelope disappeared into Nick's backpack.

Was it J.D.'s imagination, or was that backpack a little worse for wear? "Looks like you're about ready for a new bag."

Nick tossed a glance at his backpack and shrugged. "Nah, it's fine."

"You sure? Because I could buy you a new one." As long as the microwave fetched a good price.

"No, really, I'm good, Dad."

J.D. dropped his hand on Nick's shoulder. "Well, then, can you stick around? It's been a while since we had any quality time."

"Sorry, can't today. Maybe next weekend?"

"Sure. Let's give that a try." Like Elaine would ever let it happen.

Father and son shared an awkward hug. Then Nick slung his backpack over his shoulder and exited the apartment. J.D. watched and waved as he made his way down the hall. Nick never looked back to see the wave, but he felt it. At least, that's what J.D. told himself when he stepped back inside and shut the door.

He hadn't even made it back to his armchair when there was another knock. J.D. smiled. When Nick was little, he and Elaine used to joke that the boy would lose his head if it weren't for his neck. "What'd you forget, kiddo?"

But when J.D. opened the door, there was no Nick. There was no one at all. He stepped out into the hall, looked the passageway up and down, but didn't see a single sign of life.

Down by the stairs, a light bulb flickered.

3.

The next day began where yesterday had left off: more hands out demanding payment. More calls from collection agencies. The bloodsuckers were relentless. J.D. turned off the ringer on his phone, grabbed the pile of bills from the counter, and flopped down at the kitchen table.

The pile never seemed to grow smaller. And the PAST DUE stamps on the envelopes only seemed to grow bigger and brighter, more like neon signs than drawn blood. He sorted the envelopes. The car loan went straight in the trash—the repo man had taken custody of the Honda two weeks ago. No way was he paying for something that was no longer his. But the electric bill? The gas bill?

Turning down the thermostat wouldn't be enough. If he didn't want to freeze this winter, he needed to pay those suckers. Those envelopes went on the top of the pile.

J.D. sighed. He really did need to sell some furniture. Again. He'd start with the microwave.

He punched up Craigslist on his phone. Placing an ad should be straightforward, right? But after staring at the screen, turning his phone this way and that, J.D. gave up.

He texted Nick. *You remember how you set up those ads for me on Craigslist? Your old man could use some help doing it for himself.*

He was wrestling the microwave power cord out of the socket when his phone's text alert pinged.

What for?

J.D. typed with his thumb. *Selling more stuff.*

Moments later, his phone played Nick's ringtone. "Hey, kid. This really didn't require a phone call."

"Dad, do you need back some of the money you gave me? 'Cause you can have it."

"No, that money is for you. Don't give it a second thought."

"Then what's the deal with Craigslist?"

"I thought I'd sell a few things. It's not a big deal."

"Dad, you only have a few things. What's left to sell?"

"The microwave."

"You're selling your *microwave*? How are you going to eat?"

J.D. shook his head and threw a glance at the ceiling. *Kids.* "I still have an oven and a stovetop." He left out the part about needing to pay the gas bill so he could keep using them.

"Are you sure you don't need any of that money back?"

"I'm *sure*. You know, I am the father here. It's my job to worry about you, not the other way around."

"If you say so." Nick said those four words exactly like his mother would.

J.D. couldn't stop the sharpness in his voice. "Look, when I'm old and decrepit and ready for a nursing home, then you can worry about me. For now, I just need a crash course in Craigslist."

"Geez, Dad, chill. I just don't want you to end up homeless—especially because you gave me money you needed for yourself."

"You're right. I'm sorry. I promise I'm not going to end up homeless. I just want some beer money." How effortlessly that lie rolled off his tongue.

"Okay. Just text me the deets. I'll get the ad up this afternoon."

J.D. shook his head. "No, sir. I'm not asking you to do it for me. I'm asking you to teach me to do it myself."

"Dad, really, it'll be easier and faster if I just—"

"No. If you feed a man a fish—" J.D.'s phone beeped with another incoming call. "Sorry. Gimme a sec."

Caller ID announced the call was from DEBT COLLECT. J.D. sent the call to voicemail. He'd delete the message later.

He clicked back to Nick's call. "Sorry, where were we?"

"Something about fish?"

"Right. If you feed a man a fish, he eats for a day. If you teach a man to fish, he will eat for a lifetime."

"What?"

J.D. shook his head. "Never mind. Just tell me how to place the ad."

Nick took a breath. "Fine. Here's what you do—"

"Wait, wait. Let me grab a pen and write this down."

Nick made a noise that sounded like a snort. Or maybe it was a chuckle. "Tell you what. I'll type something up and email it to you. Would that work?"

"Like a charm. Thanks, kid."

J.D. ended the call and dropped his phone on the pile of bills, still screaming his name in bold letters. The blood red FINAL NOTICE and PAST DUE stamps danced in front of him, calling to him, taunting him. *You'll never pay us off. There's so many more where we came from.* His shoulders tensed, the weight of a thousand debt collectors crouching on them.

Another knock on the door. Now what? Kurt again? A collection agent? Someone other bloodsucker who wanted a chunk of J.D.'s flesh? Couldn't they all just leave him alone? It's not like his answer was suddenly going to change.

J.D. took a breath and held it, remaining still even as his lungs began to ache.

One more knock and then the swish of something sliding under the door.

J.D. waited until the footsteps faded before investigating. A business card. That was new.

Morton Deces

FINAL SOLUTION

FINANCIAL SERVICES

We make your money problems go away.

"Yeah, right." J.D. flipped the card into the trash. Even as a kid, he hadn't believed in fairy tales.

That evening, as J.D. scrubbed the last of the tomato sauce stains from the microwave, another knock on the door made his breath catch. The same crisp knock, the same rhythm, as earlier. *Not again.*

J.D.'s eyes focused on the envelopes stacked on his counter, every one with an unmistakable FINAL NOTICE or PAST DUE stamp. The stack had grown by three with today's mail delivery. It would only get bigger tomorrow. Maybe he should hear what these financial services people had to say. It didn't cost anything to listen.

J.D. opened the door on the second knock.

The man in the hall was tall, thin, and angular. He wore a dark suit, crisp white shirt, and perfectly symmetrical blood-red tie. One of his bony hands held a shiny black briefcase. He held out the other. "Sir, I'm Morton Deces from Final Solutions Financial Services. How are you today?"

"Fine." J.D. shook the man's hand, trying not to wince at the cold clamminess.

"May I come in?"

J.D. glanced over his shoulder.

"This won't take long." Deces leaned in and dropped his voice to a hiss-like whisper. "I find money matters are best discussed in private."

J.D. stepped back so the man could pass.

Deces settled himself at the table, his briefcase opening with a snap. Taking out a legal pad and pen, he slid the case to the side and gestured at the opposite seat. "Please."

J.D. slid into the chair, suddenly a stranger in his own apartment.

"So," Deces began, pen poised above the pad, "tell me about your finances."

J.D.'s gut tied itself into an intricate knot. Give his financial information to a complete stranger? He might be desperate, but he wasn't stupid. "Before we get to that, I have a few questions."

Deces set down his pen and clenched then unclenched his fists. "Of course."

J.D. leaned forward. "First off, how did you get my name?"

"I don't have your name. You haven't shared it with me yet."

"So you knocked on my door by chance?"

"I wouldn't say *chance*. I'm a door-to-door salesman. I knock on many doors."

"You sell financial planning door to door?"

"Not financial planning, no. That requires money. We assist individuals on the other end of the financial spectrum."

"But door to door?"

There was something practiced about the way Deces shrugged. "I'm an old-fashioned man doing an old-fashioned job."

J.D. let that sit. "Exactly what financial services does your firm offer?"

Deces pulled a shiny brochure out of his briefcase and slid it across the table. J.D. kept his focus on Deces's face.

"We provide a wide variety of services, which allows us to cater to each client's individual needs."

"And your rates?"

"Competitive." Deces must have seen J.D.'s face fall. "But flexible."

"Define *flexible*."

Deces leaned back in his chair and tented his long fingers. "We have occasionally had a client . . . fall short. For them, we have restructured their payment plans, or accepted payment of a . . . different kind."

J.D.'s gaze shifted over Deces's shoulder, magnetized to the screaming tower of bills on his counter. "Do you ever repossess or use collection agencies?"

"In extreme cases, yes, unfortunately, we have. But those cases have been rare. We try to work with our clients to avoid such . . . unhappy endings."

J.D. had seen enough unhappy endings. He tore his gaze away from the bills. "So what can you do for me?"

Deces smiled. No—he grinned. It wasn't pretty. There was something off about it, like it was too big for his face. It reminded J.D. of the Cheshire cat. That damn thing had given him nightmares for months as a child.

The pile of bills with their blood-red stamps is scarier.

Deces picked up his pen. He clicked the button, a sound that silenced the bills for just a second. "Why don't we start with your name?"

J.D. cleared his throat, his focus concentrated on Deces's pen. "Jason Donovan, but everyone calls me J.D."

Deces scribbled on his pad, the scritch and scratch of his pen filling the air. "And what would you say is your most immediate financial need, Mr. Donovan?"

"Getting my life back."

The financial planner raised an eyebrow, Spock-style, so J.D. explained his situation. As he talked, his hands shook.

Deces put his hand on J.D.'s. It felt chilly, like he'd been holding an ice pack. "Mr. Donovan, I assure you, yours is not the first tale of woe I have heard this week—or today. Many in this community are in your exact situation. Hardship is no stranger around here."

That was true. The town had been dying since the plant closed. Those who could move away, had. Everyone else, J.D. included, struggled to make ends meet.

Deces pulled his hand back, flipped to a new page of his pad, and scribbled quickly. Turning the page to face J.D., he said, "This is what I can do for you." He walked J.D. through his plan, item by item.

By the time Deces left, the sun had set, a full moon was rising, and J.D. had signed on the dotted line.

4.

J.D. hadn't even made his morning coffee yet and already he had two potential buyers in a bidding war for his microwave. The Craigslist ad had been up for all of—J.D. checked his watch—16 hours. "Who knew a beat up old microwave would be so popular?" he mumbled to himself. At least he'd have some money to tide him over until that Deces guy made some headway on J.D.'s debts.

Assuming that he did make headway on J.D.'s debts.

As he listened to the bubble and drip of brewing coffee, J.D. studied the pile of bills on his counter. Was it his imagination, or did it look a little smaller this morning, the red ink on the envelopes duller and less urgent?

He shook his head clear of the illusion. He didn't owe a penny less this morning than he did last night. In fact, he probably owed a few dollars more, what with compound interest and all.

The ready light on the coffee maker clicked on. J.D. poured himself a cup and took a long sip. What were the odds that the tall pale man who knocked on his door last night with the answer to all his prayers would actually deliver?

J.D. was willing to let Deces prove his mettle, but he longed for a Plan B. But what on Earth would that plan be? It's not like J.D. had options. It was Deces or nothing. Worse than nothing—eviction and homelessness.

Mid-text to Buyer #1, his phone rang. The wicked witch refrain. J.D. answered without thinking. Only after he'd pressed the green button did it occur to him that he might have made a mistake. If Elaine had found out about the money he gave Nick—

"J.D.?" His ex sounded tinny and, surprisingly, not angry.

"Elaine?"

"I just wanted to say thank you."

J.D.'s thoughts raced. What had he done?

"The check was delivered today. You didn't have to pay everything all at once, and you certainly didn't have to include the extra."

"Yeah, well—"

"I just wanted you to know that we—me and Nick—we appreciate it. I . . . thank you."

She hung up before J.D. could say anything more. Not that he had anything to add. His brain was still catching up.

Deces! He'd said the first step was settling J.D.'s debts. But that was *last night*. How had he managed to take care of everything so quickly?

J.D. shook his head. *Don't look a gift horse in the mouth, man.*

His phone pinged with a text alert. Buyer #2 had upped his offer.

J.D. sat on it. Basking in the bright sun shining through the window, he drank his coffee—savored it—and then texted both buyers. *Sorry, the microwave is no longer available.*

Day by day, the mail brought more good news. Each afternoon, his box contained another envelope or two with a statement that read PAID IN FULL. The harassing phone calls from the collection agencies dwindled into silence.

Breathing freer than he had in months, J.D. eased open his purse strings. He traded his dollar ramen dinners for boxed mac and cheese and replaced his worn-out sneakers with a new pair instead of adding yet another layer of insoles. He even bought himself a new shirt—button-down—and a new pair of slacks. Garbed in his new purchases, he splurged on a bowl of cioppino at the fancy Italian place on the other side of town. His steps grew lighter, springier. He spent time admiring the autumn leaves. More than once, he found himself smiling at passersby. And finally, finally, he was getting nibbles on his job applications. To celebrate, J.D. allowed himself a beer at the local bar.

Back in his flush days, J.D. had spent more than his fair share of time and money at Benji's. He'd even had his own stool. It had been so long since he'd darkened the bar's door that his seat surely belonged to someone else now. But everything else about the place seemed unchanged, familiar and welcoming— the square modular building that was never meant to be the permanent fixture it became, the wood paneled walls, the decorative beer signs and mirrors, the pool table angled in the corner. Just an everyday no muss, no fuss watering hole.

J.D. took in the scene and smiled. Roy, the joint's owner, greeted J.D. with a wave from behind the bar. "Howdy, stranger. Long time, no see."

J.D. answered with a nod. What could he say? Roy spoke the truth.

"What can I getcha?"

"A beer." J.D. fingered the few bills in his pocket. "The cheapest you got."

Roy obliged. J.D. tossed the money on the bar and took his drink to a small round table along the wall. He'd gotten his money's worth—the beer was the worst he'd ever tasted—but sitting there nursing it gave him a feeling of contentment that he'd forgotten he'd ever known.

He sauntered home under the light of the full moon, whistling an old Bob Seger tune, the stars smiling on him from high in the sky. He fumbled with the key, letting out a whoop when he finally managed to get the door open. Humming more Seger, he groped for the switch.

The light revealed Deces sitting at the table, still somehow in shadow. Eerie—sharp, angular, ghostly pale, long and slim like that Slenderman character.

"Mr. Donovan." Deces bowed his head. "I am so glad you're home. We have some business to discuss."

"Now?" J.D. blinked. "Wait. How the hell did you get in?"

"Your landlord was most helpful."

"Kurt? He had no right!"

"That is not for me to say. I will say that once I gave Mr. Howell a check covering six months of your full rent plus interest, he proved to be most accommodating."

J.D. didn't know what to say to that. But he'd definitely have a word with Kurt in the morning. In the meantime, he needed to deal with the creepy stranger at his kitchen table. "Do we have to do this now? It's not exactly normal business hours."

"Yes, I'm afraid we do have to do this now. Please." Deces gestured for J.D. to sit.

J.D. flopped into a chair. He tried to focus, but the beer and the late hour made it difficult.

"As you know, Mr. Donovan, we advanced quite a bit of money on your account."

"Yes, I do know. Thank you. I can't tell you how much—"

Deces brushed away J.D.'s words. "It's time to make a payment, Mr. Donovan."

"A payment? I never received a statement."

"Oh, no. We don't use statements." Deces leaned forward, his voice a hiss. "We take care of such business in person. That's what allows us to be flexible."

"But I haven't found work yet."

"Then perhaps you can name a proxy. Someone to stand up for you."

J.D. didn't hesitate. Only one person still had his back: Gallagher, his old foreman at the plant.

Deces wrote down the name. "And where might I find Mr. Gallagher?"

"You mean his address?"

Deces nodded, a slow methodical motion.

"I don't know his exact address, but he lives over on Washington, between Hayes and Grant. You can't miss it. It's the only yellow clapboard house on a block of brick bungalows."

Another nod. "Thank you, Mr. Donovan. I will see you again."

Gallagher's death was front page in the morning paper.

J.D. barely made it to the bathroom before his breakfast came back up.

When he'd wiped his mouth, rinsed the sink, and taken a few calming breaths, J.D.

returned to the table. He picked up the paper again with shaking hands.

The article was more eulogy than news report. It named Gallagher's family—a daughter, a son, three grandchildren, and a wife of thirty years—and described his history in the community: the Lions Club, Boy Scouts, Little League, and VFW.

None of it told J.D. what he wanted to know: had Gallagher saved his old employee's ass before he died?

5.

The next month, J.D. was ready. He'd gained some momentum with interviews and prospects, but Gallagher's death had goosed him. J.D. worked a little harder selling himself, made a couple of extra phone calls instead of waiting for the phone to ring. And while he still heard more no's than yes's, he'd ended up with more work than he'd had in months, thanks to the demand for holiday help. The resulting cash sat in an envelope on the table.

Deces arrived after sundown, the full moon starting its ascent in the sky.

Deces laughed as he fingered the money. "My dear Mr. Donovan. I applaud the effort, but this is not nearly enough."

"How much more do you need?"

Deces shrugged. "Another name would suffice. Mr. Gallagher was most obliging. Perhaps you can refer another coworker?"

"So you did talk with Glen?" J.D. sagged, his insides suddenly hollow. "Before he—"

"I did, indeed." Deces nodded, his expression stony and bland. "His passing was most unfortunate. You have my condolences."

"Thank you." Deces's words sounded more formal than heartfelt to J.D., but he would take what he could get. He bit back the urge to ask what happened. The idea that Deces would harm Gallagher, that he would kill an innocent man, over someone else's debt was ridiculous. Even loan sharks wouldn't go that far. The whole thing—it had to be a freak coincidence. Didn't it?

The two men sat in silence, the air heavy with expectation. J.D. traced the grain of the tabletop. Another coworker? He could count on one hand the ones who were left. They were not his favorite people, and he hadn't been one of theirs.

Deces watched, a hawk studying its prey. Finally, he tapped his watch. "Mr. Donovan, I'm afraid I need a name."

J.D. shook his head. "I can't. Really. There isn't anyone—"

"Now, Mr. Donovan."

J.D. huffed. After a moment of thought, he named the best of the worst. "Charlie, I guess. Charlie Simmons."

"Thank you." Deces swept the envelope off the table and made his exit.

J.D. sighed with relief as the door shut.

With Deces gone, J.D. wilted into his armchair, something sharp but vague nagging at him. The feeling poked at him until his limbs twitched. After an excruciating hour, he pushed himself out of his chair and dragged himself down to Benji's. Maybe a beer at the bar would settle his nerves.

The door slammed shut behind him, rattling the windows of the modular building. In the din of conversation and games of pool, no one seemed to notice. J.D. made his way to the bar and his favorite stool. The shelves behind the bar were dotted with shiny plastic holly leaves. In the mirror, J.D. could see a fully decorated tree in the back corner. No presents, though, under the tree or in J.D.'s budget. Yet.

The bartender was new. A woman. To J.D., she seemed young—younger than him, at least—but she moved with a confidence that he only ever dreamed of having.

He waved her over. "Beer, please. Whatever you've got on tap."

"Olsberg okay?"

J.D. nodded.

The bartender slid a cocktail napkin in front of him and then set a glass of foamy beer on it. "That'll be $5.50, please."

J.D. slid his wallet from his back pocket. "So where's Roy tonight?"

"Taking some much-deserved time off."

"Good for him. Is this going to be a regular thing? Roy at home with his feet up, you tending the bar?"

The bartender nodded. "More like Roy handles the days and I handle the nights, but yeah, we're giving it a try."

J.D. dropped eight dollars on the bar. "Keep the change. I'm J.D., by the way."

"Lisa." She took the money, acknowledging the generous tip with raised eyebrows and an impressed frown.

They continued the small talk, trading abbreviated biographies while J.D. nursed his drink. It turned out that J.D. had worked the line with Lisa's father, who had retired to Arizona a few months before the plant closed.

"How's your old man doing down there?" J.D. asked.

"Counting the days until his little girl finally joins him."

J.D. took a sip. "So why hasn't she?"

"If she could afford it, she would. I'm almost there, though. Say what you will about this being a dying town, the bar scene is as flush as it gets."

J.D. raised his glass. "To bars and collection agencies—the vultures picking over the town's carcass."

Lisa grimaced. Shaking her head, she went to help another customer.

J.D. focused on his beer. He drank in silence, eavesdropping on snippets of conversation around him. No one was having a good day.

He threw back the last swallow. The butterflies had settled. It was time for him to go home.

"Donovan!"

J.D. turned to find Charlie Simmons behind him, pool cue in one hand, empty beer bottle in the other, anger in every feature of his face. "Charlie. Buy you a drink?"

"A drink? That's the best you can do, you son of a bitch?" Charlie reached past J.D. and plopped the bottle on the bar. A second later, Charlie's fist landed hard on J.D.'s cheekbone.

J.D. sat stunned and mute, his cheek stinging, his brain struggling to compute what happened, struggling to compose a response.

Charlie had no such problem. "Who do you think you are, anyway? Giving my details out without my permission. The least you could have done was ask."

That solved that mystery. "So Deces called you already, huh?"

"Called? No. Bastard ambushed me outside my kid's karate class. OUTSIDE MY KID'S CLASS, Donovan."

"I'm sorry, Charlie, I didn't think he'd be so on the ball. I came here tonight to give you a heads up." A nit poked at the back of J.D.'s brain—*How did Deces know where to go?*—but J.D. shoved it aside.

Charlie seemed to soften just a tiny bit. "What does he want?"

J.D. took a deep breath. "He's going to ask if you'll vouch for me."

"Vouch for you? Why the hell would I do that? Why would you need me to?"

J.D. fiddled with the beer bottle that Charlie had abandoned, spinning it with a finger, picking at the label. "He—his company—helped me with some money stuff. I'm trying to pay him back, but I can't quite swing the full payments yet. He just wants to know that I'm good for the rest of it. That's all."

"Again, why would I do that? What made you think I would?"

J.D. pushed the bottle away. "There aren't many of us left. And it's not like I could ask Gallagher."

Charlie nodded, his expression almost contrite. "Yeah, man. I'm sorry. I know the two of you were close."

"Thanks." J.D. scooted to the edge of his stool. "Look, I know we're not friends. But you coached Nick in youth hockey, and you were good to him. I was hoping that you'd do it for his sake. Think of it as a . . . a Christmas gift."

Charlie motioned to Lisa for another drink. "Nick's a good kid. He's got talent. And a strong work ethic."

J.D. kept his mouth shut. What could he say? His son got both of those things from his mother.

Lisa pushed a brown bottle toward Charlie.

He picked it up and took a swig. "Put it on J.D.'s tab, sweetheart." Another swig. "I'll say this for you, Donovan. You always did play by the rules." Charlie took a long drink. "I'm not saying I'll do this thing for you, but if I do, you'll owe me. And more than a drink, too."

J.D. nodded and held out his hand. "Of course."

Charlie refused the handshake, taking his beer back to the pool table and calling for the next game.

6.

J.D. waited on tenterhooks for days, his bruised and sore cheek a reminder of what hung over his head. He replayed his confrontation with Charlie on a loop. He rehashed every word, examined the nuance of every syllable, studied the memory of every blink, every swallow, with the studiousness of those forensic scientists he used to watch on TV. Every time he played it through, he came up with a different answer.

Would Charlie vouch for him? He had no reason to. J.D.'s appeal to Charlie's history as a youth coach had been little more than a grasp at a flimsy straw. Back in the good old days at the factory, their relationship—if you could call it that—was of the "live and let live" variety, a wide berth being the key to its success. Sending Deces in his direction slammed that gap closed, and as Charlie's anger the other night showed, he was not happy about that. Charlie was still just as likely to throw J.D. under the bus as help him.

Friday night, J.D. wanted to watch the Red Wings. The game, though, was an ESPN exclusive, and he'd given up his cable subscription ages ago. He still couldn't afford more than the free digital antenna channels, so off to the bar he went. With any luck, Charlie would be there, and J.D. could get his answer. He grabbed a tenner from this month's money envelope and headed for Benji's.

But luck wasn't with J.D. that night. No ESPN on the bar TV and no Charlie, either. Not at the pool table he usually hustled. Not at the corner table he usually occupied. Not at any seat at the bar. Not even in the dingy men's room in the back.

J.D. searched the room for a familiar face, someone who might know where Charlie was, but came up empty. He hoisted himself onto a stool at the bar. Lisa was on duty.

He ordered his usual cheap beer. "You haven't seen Charlie Simmons around lately, have ya?"

The bartender shook her head. "Haven't seen him all week. Not since the two of you had your, um, conversation."

J.D. frowned. "Thanks."

The bar door swung open and banged shut. Lisa nodded at the newcomer. "Ask Gray. He might know."

"Might know what?" Gray sidled up next to J.D. Whether Gray was his given name or a nickname because of his coat and his hair's stormy color, J.D. never knew. From the smell of him, Gray had already gotten a few under his belt. But then, J.D. wasn't sure Gray was ever sober.

"Where Charlie's been." The bartender put a little flirt in her voice. "It's not like him to leave me alone so long."

Gray grinned. "Guess you'll have to settle for me, then." The grin vanished. A pall fell over him as he continued. "Charlie's in the hospital. Been there since Tuesday? Wednesday? Something like that."

A chill went down J.D.'s spine. "The hospital? Anything serious?"

The bartender slid a shot in front of Gray. He picked it up and downed it in a single move. "I'll say. Docs can't figure out what's wrong. They've been running tests and doing scans. They've taken enough blood to feed an army of vampires. Everything comes back normal. Except Charlie—" He slammed the shot glass on the bar. "—ain't normal."

Lisa slid another shot in front of him, and Gray downed that one too. "They're talking about exploratory surgery, cutting him from stem to stern and poking around to see if they can find anything."

What kind *of anything?* J.D. wondered.

"Jesus." The bartender looked as pale as J.D. felt.

J.D. tightened his grip on his beer. "What happened? He seemed fine last week."

"Sure did." Gray nodded. "Kicked my ass at the pool table, just like always. Heard he tore you a new one, too. Then Tuesday, completely out of the blue, he started wheezing, his lungs sounding like a baby rattle. Less than an hour later, he clutched his chest and collapsed."

"Pneumonia?"

Gray shrugged. "That's what everyone thought at first. That or a heart attack. But the usual treatments had no effect. Charlie's been in and out of consciousness ever since. Cora said he keeps mumbling something about a suit."

"A suit? Are they being sued?"

Gray shrugged. "No idea. I mean, he did have an appointment that night, and it coulda been with a lawyer, but I don't see how. Nothing about this makes any sense."

An appointment but probably not a lawsuit . . . A suit of clothing? J.D.'s insides dropped out. "Well, Charlie's a tough son of a bitch. If anyone can pull through, it's him."

Gray called for another shot and then continued as if J.D. hadn't said a word. "Cora's beside herself with worry."

"Give her my best." J.D. laid his hand on Gray's shoulder. "Let her know I'll be praying for her and for Charlie."

He trembled all the way home. Even a hot shower and cranked up thermostat didn't make the shivers go away.

J.D. returned to Benji's the next night and the night after that and the night after that. He became more regular than the regulars. He always sat at the bar, but never on the same stool twice in a row and always nursing a single glass of seltzer each night.

Pool table gossip kept J.D. informed of Charlie's progress—or rather, his lack of progress. If anything, he'd gotten worse. Doctors referred to his condition as a coma but remained baffled by the specifics. They said it was like his body had aged three decades overnight, without any organic reason for doing so. He was breathing only by virtue of a ventilator. Day by day, he looked more and more like a mummy, all withered and bent and twisted, like the life force was being sucked out of him. The docs couldn't find a case like it anywhere in their medical literature.

The regulars at the bar, on the other hand, had plenty of theories. It was something in the air, or the water, or the soil, a pollutant left behind by the factory. It was the bite of an invasive species of insect. It was poison, administered by a representative of some shady real estate conglomerate trying to buy up the whole town. It was a biological weapon, a virus, cooked up by a foreign government to destroy America. The longer Charlie was hospitalized, the more outlandish the theories became. Around and around they went, masking their worry with "research" while Charlie declined. The gossips never did get around to blaming aliens or the president, but they were certainly well on their way there.

On New Year's Eve, a few minutes before midnight, Charlie passed, his diagnosis still a mystery and his body, unrecognizable. Lisa broke the news the next day, before J.D. had a chance to slide onto his stool. He skipped his usual beer or seltzer that night in favor of a shot of Charlie's favorite whiskey.

Lisa joined him. "To Charlie."

They clinked glasses and threw back the firewater.

"Funeral's next week—Thursday," Lisa said. "Everyone will be gathering here after."

J.D. made a vow to go. Sure, that Thursday was a full moon, but Deces would have to wait. J.D.'s meager payment would be just as good on Friday morning.

7.

The bar was packed the night of Charlie's funeral. The plastic holly leaves from Christmas still hung behind the bar, seemingly duller than they were a month ago, as if they, too, were in mourning. The Christmas tree had been pulled out and replaced with a large easel displaying a giant portrait of Charlie. The portrait looked like a favorite family photo, taken a backyard barbecue. Charlie was looking at the camera, a smile on his face and a beer in his hand, raised in a toast to the photographer. As mourners passed the easel, they raised their drinks in return.

The room buzzed with conversation, and every conversation was the same. Everyone had a Charlie story to tell. Most of the stories were about pool hustles or drunken escapades, stories that put weak, forced smiles on the faces of Cora and her kids. But a few were about the favor of a loyal friend—a loan for emergency car repairs, help building bunkbeds for a surprise Christmas present, companionship during a cancer scare, commiseration after a miscarriage. Those stories drew bright teary smiles from the Simmons family.

J.D., seated at the end of the bar nursing his usual beer, kept his story to himself. It wouldn't make anyone smile anyway.

Pounding on the pool table broke through the din of the crowd. The din dwindled to a gentle murmur. A fork pinged against the side of a glass. J.D. turned and saw Mal, one of Charlie's buddies from the factory, standing on the pool table.

Mal stretched his right arm high with a beer glass in his hand. "A toast!"

Glasses rose throughout the crowd, like the wave at a baseball stadium. J.D. slid off his stool and lifted his near-empty beer bottle.

"To Charlie," Mal declared. "May he be pocketing the 8 ball in the great pool table in the sky!"

The crowd answered as one. "To Charlie!"

J.D. scooted back onto his stool and waved for another drink.

A bottle slid across the bar, right into his hand. Someone sidled up on J.D.'s left. A chill washed over him.

"Mr. Donovan, did you forget our appointment?" Deces could not have sounded more like a scolding parent if he tried.

J.D. didn't look up from his drink. "I'm afraid so."

Deces placed a cold hand on J.D.'s elbow. "Then why don't we retire to your abode so we can take care of business?"

J.D. yanked his arm away. "No. I'm staying here. I'm mourning a friend. You'll get your money. but not tonight."

"Ah, but I'm afraid it must be tonight. Those are the terms of our agreement."

J.D. took a swig of beer. "What happened to all that flexibility you promised? Does it really make all that much difference if you get your money at 9 am instead of 9 pm?"

"As a matter of fact, it does." Deces grabbed J.D.'s beer with two fingers and placed it out of J.D.'s reach. He gestured toward the door. "Shall we?"

As J.D. rose to reach for his drink, Lisa the Bartender slid to their end of the bar. She placed her hands on her hips. "Is there a problem here?"

Deces dropped his hand and bowed his head. "No, ma'am. Not at all."

"Actually, we're at a bit of standstill." J.D. grabbed his beer and fell back onto his seat. "I owe Mr. Deces some money, and he's insisting I get it for him right this very minute."

Lisa shrugged. "Surely a few dollars can wait until morning. This is a wake, after all."

J.D. turned toward Deces and raised his eyebrows.

Deces's cordiality became condescension. "I'm afraid, young lady, the arrangement is not as informal as Mr. Donovan implies."

Lisa narrowed her eyes and crossed her arms, her hands folded into fists. Her clenched jaw twitched. Not even rude, handsy customers earned that level of ire. "Frankly, sir, I don't give a damn about your 'arrangement.' I do give a damn about my boys, one of whom is being mourned here tonight. Now, if J.D. says he's good for it, he's good for it, and you'd do well to take him at his word. You'll get your damn money tomorrow."

J.D. bit his cheek, keeping his eyes on Deces.

Deces, meanwhile, stared at Lisa, his features sharper and colder than J.D. had ever seen them. Lisa stared right back.

Deces leaned forward, his hand sliding across the bar toward the bartender. "Ma'am, is my understanding correct? Are you vouching for Mr. Donovan here?"

J.D. held up his hand. "No, she's not."

Lisa leaned back on her heels. "Yes, I am."

J.D. sharpened his tone. "NO. She's not." He stared at Lisa, hoping she had enough telepathy to pick up his warning.

She didn't. In a tone as sharp as J.D.'s, she repeated, "YES. I am."

Deces slapped the bar and nodded. "Very well." He held out his hand to J.D. "Until next time, then, Mr. Donovan."

J.D. turned his back to Deces, bile burning his throat. He downed the rest of his beer, planting it on the bar with a loud clunk. Bitterness clung to the back of his mouth. He stared at Lisa. "What were you thinking, vouching for me like that?"

The bartender stood with her arms crossed and a fierce expression on her face. She didn't even blink. "Me? What about you? What are you doing business with a creep like him for?"

"Didn't really have much of a choice. You did, though." J.D. reached across the bar and grabbed Lisa's arm. "You have no idea what you just stepped into. You've got to take it back."

Lisa scowled and yanked her arm out of J.D.'s grasp. "Why would I do that?"

J.D. took a deep breath. What could he tell her? That she'd end up like Charlie? Like Gallagher? She'd never believe him. Hell, J.D. had trouble believing it. And if he did talk her out of it, what would happen to him? To his deal with Deces? Every muscle cringed at the idea of going back to life before. "I don't want you to get hurt."

She slid him a beer. "Don't you worry your pretty little head. I can take care of myself."

"I have no doubt. But this Deces guy—"

"Look, you needed someone to vouch for you. I did. End of story."

"Not quite. Deces has a habit of . . . following up. And he's not very nice about it."

"Look, J.D., I appreciate the concern. I've got pepper spray and a black belt. And I promise to be extra careful. Okay, Mom?"

J.D. frowned and took a swig of his drink.

Lisa walked away, shaking her head in disappointment. It was a gesture J.D. knew well, thanks to his ex-wife.

His gut told him to force the issue, to warn her again but with more vigor. The words lodged in his throat. He chugged the drink and one more in quick succession, but neither jarred the words loose or quieted the churning in his stomach. What the hell was he supposed to do now?

8.

The next morning, the opening riff of "Solsbury Hill" played over and over, pulling J.D. out of sleep and into a sluggish half-wakefulness. He fumbled for the phone, knocking it on the floor. The song's baseline pounded in his head. A minute or two later, the tune played from under his bed.

He felt around for the phone and answered the call with a groan.

"Dad?

"Hey, kid." J.D. hoped he sounded better than he felt.

"You okay? You sound awful."

So much for that hope. "Just a little hungover. What's going on? Aren't you in school?"

"Yeah. It's my lunch period."

Lunch? J.D. looked at the clock. How had it gotten so late? He shook his head. His brain felt like it was about to explode.

"So it is. How've you been? I haven't heard much from you lately."

"Yeah, I know. I'm sorry. I've been busy with school and hockey and stuff."

"What kind of stuff? Inquiring minds want to know." J.D. tried to make the last sentence sound like a joke. A bad dad joke was better than his son hearing the lump of tears in his throat. Those small details in Nick's life. Who knew they'd take up so much room in a broken heart?

Someone in the background of Nick's call yelled for him.

"Look, Dad, I don't have a lot of time. I just ... I'm worried about Mom."

"What do you mean? What's wrong?" J.D. left out the *And why do you think I can do anything about it?*

"I don't know. She's just not herself. I can't really explain it."

"Have you talked to her about it?"

"I tried. She told me not to worry. She said it was nothing."

J.D. sighed. "Kid, if there's one thing I know about your mother, it's that she can take care of herself. That doesn't mean it's always going to be good times. Maybe she is going through something right now, but she'll get through it. I promise. You just worry about you."

Nick's disappointment radiated through the phone. "Yeah, okay. Thanks."

Just like he was gone. J.D. stared at the screen, hoping Nick would call back with one more question. He considered calling Nick and asking for more about Elaine, but Nick clearly had a full life of his own. The big numbers on the phone reminded J.D. of how much of the day he'd already lost.

He fell back onto his pillow. When was the last time he'd drunk so much or been this hungover? What the hell had he done? He stumbled into the bathroom, threw cold water on his face, and tossed back a couple of Advil. Wet but no more awake, he made his way to the kitchen and his coffee machine. Thank God he hadn't sold that. Cup of joe in hand, he flopped into his chair.

His mouse friend appeared on the counter, sniffing with curiosity.

J.D. pointed his finger at it. "Not a word out of you."

The mouse scurried away.

As he sipped his coffee, J.D. wracked his sore head, pulling his memory reluctantly through the events of the previous day. By the time his recollections made it through Charlie's funeral, the painkiller had kicked in and his mind was starting to clear. What was it Gray had said? Charlie had an appointment and fell sick right after. And he'd been mumbling about a suit. That appointment. It had to have been with Deces. Before that, it was Gallagher. He'd met with Deces and then died.

A chill raced up J.D.'s spine, spread to every nerve ending. His coffee cup fell from his grip, crashing to the ground.

Lisa vouched for me last night.

I said I'd have the money to Deces by 9 am.

It's after 11 now.

He stuffed ten dollars in his pocket and grabbed his coat. Tripping over a chair in his rush, he headed out, spilled coffee be damned.

Roy found J.D. huddled and shivering on the stoop when he opened the front door. He waved J.D. inside. "Donovan, you're here awfully early. You tryin' to freeze to death or something?"

J.D. jumped to his feet and rubbed the feeling back into his ass. "I'm looking for Lisa. What time does she get in?"

The bar owner frowned and shook his head. "She's not. She called in sick. Left me a message last night."

J.D.'s mouth went dry. Hungover like him sick, or dying like Charlie sick? He slid onto a stool and tapped the bar for a drink.

"Never took you for a day drinker." Roy grabbed a bottle of J.D.'s usual and pushed it across the bar.

"Hair of the dog, my friend." J.D. held the bottle in a toast before taking a swig. Bottle back on the bar, he fiddled with the label. "So Lisa, is she . . .?"

Roy snorted. "You two start dating and not tell anyone?"

"No, it's not that. It's just . . . something happened last night, and I want to make sure she's okay. That's all."

Instantly, Roy was all business—straight posture, straighter expression. "Tell me."

J.D. hesitated.

Roy put both hands on the bar. "I don't tolerate any shit in my bar, Donovan. What the hell happened?"

J.D. took a deep breath and gave Roy the short version of Deces's visit. "Boundaries are not something this guy seems to understand. I want to make sure he didn't hassle Lisa after I left."

Roy nodded. He pulled his cellphone from his shirt pocket and dialed. Handing the phone to J.D., he said, "Ask her yourself."

Six rings later, Lisa's voicemail picked up. J.D. tried to sound casual. "Hey, Lisa. It's J.D. from the bar. I just wanted to make sure you got home okay. Give Roy a call when you can. Thanks."

He handed the phone back to Roy, thanked him, and trudged back home. He took the long way, hoping to settle his nerves. By the time he reached his door, he knew the only way to ease his worry was to see Lisa for himself.

J.D. checked his phone. He'd reached his monthly limit. Welcome to the downside of pre-paid plans.

He grabbed his laptop and flipped it open. He clicked on his favorite browser, only to get an error message. Damn it. He'd cancelled his internet subscription, hadn't he? A few weeks before Deces promised to make his money problems disappear. Deces had kept that promise, but it wasn't the miracle cure that J.D. had imagined. Not by a long shot. That business card was starting to feel like a Trojan horse.

It was time for Option C. He dug his bus pass out of the drawer and headed for the library. Twenty-five minutes and one Google search later, he had Lisa's address. Two bus transfers and a short walk after that, he was at Lisa's front door.

He knocked.

No answer.

He punched the doorbell.

No answer.

He knocked again, this time calling Lisa's name.

No answer.

He leaned over to peer through the window. The crack in the blinds didn't give him a wide view, but it was enough to tell the lights were out and the TV was off. There was no movement, no signs of life.

J.D. felt eyes on his back. He turned. A curtain fluttered in the neighbor's window.

He jogged over and knocked on the door. It opened as far the chain lock would allow.

"I'm sorry to bother you." J.D. waved toward Lisa's house. "I'm a friend of Lisa's. We were at a funeral yesterday and drank away a few too many of our sorrows. I wanted to make sure she got home okay. Have you seen her?"

The gray eye that peered through the cracked door gave him a once-over.

"Please? I tried calling, but she didn't answer. She's not answering the door, either. I'm worried. That's not like her."

Another once-over. A grimace. Then, in a rough voice that could only be the result of decades of smoking, "Yeah, I saw her."

J.D. sighed, his body sagging with relief.

"But you're not going to like it."

J.D. snapped to. "What do you mean?"

"There was a man waiting for her when she got home. Tall, narrow drink of water, paler than the moonlight. They had a few words, and she went off with him, his hand on her back. She ain't been home since."

Tall, pale, narrow drink of water. That could only be Deces. J.D. muttered a thanks and backed away from the door. On the bus ride home, the pieces slid into place. The picture they created was far from pretty.

J.D. pulled out his phone. He dialed 9 and 1 and then stopped. What would he say? "Hi, I made a deal with a creepy salesman, and now I think he's killing my friends?" That sounded crazy enough in his head. It could only sound crazier if he said it out loud.

A week later, his worst fears were confirmed. Lisa's body was found in an abandoned house. The police were involved now, whether J.D. wanted it or not.

9

Sure enough, the police made their way to J.D. Their questions seemed innocuous at first: How did he know Lisa? How long had he known Lisa? What kind of relationship did he and Lisa have? Eventually, they got around to the night of Charlie's wake. J.D. answered every question truthfully, but he never mentioned Deces. It's not like they would believe him, anyway. Besides, this was his mess. He was the one who needed to clean it up.

J.D. wasn't sure what "clean it up" meant, exactly, but he knew it started with finding and confronting Deces. Final Solution must have an office of some sort, but where? Without statements, it was hard to know.

J.D. dug out the business card that started this whole rigamarole. No address there. What about that shiny brochure Deces had given him? Where had that gone?

J.D. found it stuffed in a drawer with a copy of the contract he'd signed. Odd . . . neither had an address on it. Was a contract without an address even valid? Too bad J.D. didn't have the money to find out. Damn lawyers. Not to mention, Deces didn't exactly seem like the kind of guy who would leave a *t* uncrossed or an *i* un-dotted.

So J.D. did what any self-respecting citizen of the 21st century would do. He Googled. His search results gave him no clear answer about his contract, but they did give something useful: a PO Box for Final Solution Financial Services. Finally, a place to start.

The next day, J.D. packed a lunch, filled a thermos with coffee, and staked out the post office. He spent the day sitting on the retaining wall outside the office building across the street. At 5 pm, he headed home with little more than an empty thermos, a cold butt, and a sore back. The following two days were a repeat of that first one, with one exception. In the afternoon of the third day, it began to snow. Walking home through the gentle snowfall brought an epiphany: Deces preferred to do business after dark. That probably included checking his PO Box. Those postal lobbies were open 24 hours.

At sunset on Thursday, with the sky a watercolor of pastels and the ground covered in clean white snow, J.D. set off again. No luck that night, but something about the crescent moon made him hopeful.

Each night the moon grew fuller, reminding J.D. that his time was running out. After a week, he gave up his stakeouts. The PO Box was just another ruse, another decoy to make Deces seem like a legitimate businessman. By now, the full moon was two days away, and J.D. wanted to be ready.

He knew Deces didn't want money. He wanted names. Lives, despite Deces's claim to the contrary. What J.D. didn't know was why or how Deces did the deed, nor did J.D. know how to stop him, even though he very much wanted to. Would Deces accept J.D.'s name? Was J.D. willing to make that sacrifice? Jason Donovan had the makings of an ulcer, but no answer.

Deces's crisp knock came right on time. The man was nothing if not efficient.

J.D. took a deep breath and smoothed his hair. He wiped his hands on his pants and opened the door. He waved Deces inside.

Deces wore the same suit, carried the same briefcase, as when J.D. first met him. As a matter of fact, he'd been wearing that suit every time J.D. saw him. That had to mean something, but what?

Deces held out his hand. "Your payment, Mr. Donovan?"

J.D. straightened. "Not yet. I have a question first."

Deces pulled back his hand and gave J.D. a dull stare. "Proceed."

"Where's your office? There's no address on anything."

"We have no office. That's how we keep our overhead low, and it is that low overhead that gives us the flexibility to meet our customers' needs. Flexibility that you are sorely testing, I might add. Your payment, Mr. Donovan."

"I don't have it. Not all of it, anyway."

"Then I'll need a name."

J.D. shook his head. "Nope."

"Mr. Donovan, you know how this works. You either pay me in full, or give me the name of someone who can vouch for you."

"Vouch for me? What does that mean exactly? Do they sign a piece of paper? Give you money? Because as far as I can tell, vouching for me means they die, and that is not a fair trade." J.D. balled his hands into fists and jammed them into his pockets. "Your 'flexibility' is nothing more than a fancy way of saying murder."

Deces's smile was cold. "Murder? How uncouth. We don't do anything so . . . dirty. And as I'm sure your own experience has taught you, Mr. Donovan, life is not fair. You signed a contract, and those were its terms. Now, who will it be?"

J.D. held up a finger. "One more question. How do you explain what happened to Lisa?"

"Your bartender friend? That was a tragedy, and I'm sure the police will identify the responsible party." Deces gave J.D. a pointed stare.

Was that a threat? Would Deces really go as far to frame J.D.? J.D. planted his feet. "I told you, I'm not giving you another name."

"Your friend with the bar. What is his name? Roy? Would he vouch for you?"

How did Deces know of Roy? Roy probably would vouch for J.D. All J.D. had to do was say yes, and he'd be free for another month. Free of debt and free of police suspicion. The answer called to him like a siren song.

But no, that would condemn Roy to death, and J.D. was no murderer.

Deces kept going. "Or your son, perhaps? I believe his name is Nicholas? Or maybe his mother?"

"You bastard! What gives you the right to threaten my son's life?"

"I'm simply listing your options. Each of your friends bought you one month and one month only."

What choice did J.D. have? He hadn't been a very good father, and he'd been an even worse husband, but Elaine and Nick shouldn't pay for his mistakes. If it came to down to Nick's life or his own, there was no contest.

He played the only card he could think of. "I'll call the police. Tell them what you've been doing."

Deces laughed. "My dear Mr. Donovan, I have been doing this job longer than you have been alive. I know how to deal with the police."

This time, there was no mistaking the threat in Deces's words. J.D. breathed deeply, searching for an escape route. But his only way out seemed to be through. He sat at the table and squared his shoulders. "You said that your company offered flexible repayment terms, that you're open to creative problem-solving."

Deces slid into the chair opposite and folded his hands on the table. "I did."

J.D. mimicked Deces. "So let's negotiate."

"What do you have in mind?"

"Something that will allow me to repay my debt without it costing the lives of any more of my friends."

"I see." Deces leaned back in his chair, brought his hand to his chin. To J.D., it looked like he was making a show of thinking. "You could make your payments in full each month."

"I would love to do that, but I can't guarantee that I'll be able to. Jobs are still pretty scarce around these parts."

Deces drummed his fingers on his cheek. "Hmmmm. Perhaps . . . No, that would not suit at all."

"What wouldn't?"

"Never you mind. It is something that a man such as yourself would not have the stomach for."

J.D. crossed his arms and set his jaw. "Why don't you let me make that decision?"

Deces eyed J.D. up and down. "If you insist." He leaned forward, as if conducting an interview. "Tell me about your experience in sales."

"I've only ever worked the line at the metal works."

"You have never sold anything ever in your entire life?"

J.D. considered the question. He'd had a newspaper route as a kid, but that was more delivery than sales. "The closest I ever came was selling wrapping paper, popcorn, and candy to my co-workers for my son's school fundraisers."

"So you do have experience in sales, albeit very slight."

"I suppose."

"Then here is my proposition: join the sales department at Final Solution."

J.D. blinked. "What?"

"I believe I was clear."

J.D. pushed himself to his feet. "You want me to sell your services? Go to door to door like you did when you hooked me?"

"Whether you go door to door would be your own decision, Mr. Donovan, but yes, I am offering you a chance to earn off your debt by bringing in more customers."

J.D. paced the kitchenette. "And if those customers can't make their payments? What happens to them? The same thing that happened to Gallagher and Charlie and Lisa?"

"Of course not. They would be in your shoes, Mr. Donovan."

"Who would collect their payments? Would I be responsible for that too?"

"Collections are my department."

"And if I don't get any customers, then what? You just kill everyone I know?"

Deces shrugged, his sharp angular shoulders stabbing into the air.

"I don't see how I could say yes. I can't go looking for people to put into this position."

Deces laughed. The sound was cold and hard. "My dear Mr. Donovan, you won't have to. They will come to you. Over and over again. People everywhere are killing themselves to find a way out of their self-made prisons, and nothing will stop them from getting the relief they so desperately crave. You will never want for customers. And with every one you get, your debt will shrink until you will never have need to see me again."

So these strangers would throw themselves at him and then watch their friends and family die, one by one, just as J.D. had. He paced faster, trying to get the image of Lisa lying prone and lifeless in that broken-down house out of his head. How could he possibly be party to that?

He couldn't.

J.D. returned to his chair. With a shake of his head, he rejected Deces's offer. Some jobs weren't worth the cost to the soul.

Deces leaned back again. His gaze focused on something behind J.D. He pointed in the direction of his gaze. "Is that your final answer?"

J.D. turned to see what was behind him. His mouse friend lay dead on the counter. The butterflies in J.D.'s gut fluttered in wild panic. "It is."

"I see." Deces stood and picked up his briefcase. "Then it appears I have no other choice. I will give young master Nicholas your regards."

J.D. slammed his fist onto the table. "Leave Nick out of this."

"Then his mother. What would she have to say about you, I wonder?"

"Un-unh."

Deces sat down again, his spine as straight as a flagpole. "I told you, Mr. Donovan. I am not leaving here without a name."

What little warmth had been in the apartment disappeared. Goosebumps formed on J.D.'s arm. Was this what people meant by a Sophie's choice? He could either sacrifice his own family and friends, or he could set other people up to lose theirs.

J.D. slumped in his chair. "That sales job. How would it work? Specifically, the earning off my debt part."

10.

The next afternoon, a well-taped box arrived outside J.D.'s door. Inside were all the brochures, forms, and business cards he needed to recruit more dupes to the Final Solutions scam. He left the box sitting open on his kitchen table as he went about his regular business.

That week, regular business meant two days of temp work and a job interview for a regular part-time gig. The interview didn't go so well—talking was not J.D.'s strong suit— but the bench was shallow, so maybe he still had shot. That night, though, was the highlight of his week: Nick's hockey game. J.D. got home from the interview, tore off his suit, and threw on his game gear: Red Wings sweatshirt, jeans, ball cap. Ignoring the box on his table, he scooped up his jacket and let the door slam behind him on his way out.

He knew Elaine would be sitting behind the team bench, so J.D. found a seat behind the penalty boxes. Nick wouldn't see him there, but with any luck, he'd hear him. Even if he didn't, the important thing was that J.D. was there, watching his son do what he loved.

It wasn't long before J.D. lost himself in the game, the teams rushing from one end of the ice to the other, the puck dancing from stick to stick and occasionally flying toward the net. The swish of skate blades on the ice, the clap of the puck on the sticks, the thud of bodies against the boards, the shouts of players and coaches—the game had its own soundtrack, a music that got J.D.'s heart racing and blood flowing. When the buzzer declared the end of the first period, J.D. sat down feeling like he'd run a 20-minute mile. Then Nick paused on his way off the ice and scanned the crowd. His eyes found J.D., and he waved. J.D.'s heart skipped a couple of beats.

With the teams in their locker rooms, the already-sparse crowd thinned. Refreshments must be bought. Bathrooms must be visited. J.D. stayed in his seat and watched the ebb and flow of people, a phenomenon almost as interesting as the game itself. Without meaning to, his eyes found Elaine. She wore a smart pantsuit, carried an impressive-looking leather bag, and climbed the steps with a confident spring in her step. Being on her own really had been good for her. J.D. had been right. Nick had no reason to worry about his mom.

J.D. followed Elaine's progress up the stairs and through the doorway. His heart stopped. A tall skinny figure that could only be Deces stood off to the side of the doorway. His head turned to follow Elaine as she passed by. Then he turned back, looking straight at J.D. He gave a single nod.

J.D. blinked, and Deces was gone.

Elaine.

J.D. tore up the aisle and around the concourse. He stopped short at the sight of Elaine picking through the shirts at the souvenir table. She seemed relaxed—or as relaxed as she got when she bargain hunted.

So where was Deces? J.D. scanned the crowd. Nothing. Deces was not someone who easily blended in.

With a deep breath, J.D. turned around to head back to his seat.

"J.D.? That you?"

J.D. turned back. "Elaine. How are you?"

His ex-wife smiled. "I'm well, thank you. It's good that you're here. It will mean a lot to Nick."

"I'm glad." J.D. gave her a close-lipped smile. He stood awkwardly, at a loss for else to say. He knew how to talk to wicked witch Elaine, but this kinder, gentler Elaine threw him off balance. He had no idea how to handle her. "Well, it was good seeing you." He shook her hand and headed back to his seat.

So had Deces really been there? Or had J.D. imagined it? By the time the second period started, J.D. had a headache from trying to figure it out.

A little more than an hour later, Nick's game ended in a tie, and J.D. still had no answers.

The next morning, J.D. startled awake in a tangle of sheets on a sweat-stained pillow, certain that Deces stood at the end of his bed. It took a solid 30 seconds for his heart and breathing to calm, and a good minute longer for his brain to accept that J.D. was, in fact, alone.

He jumped at the sound of his phone. The temp agency. He'd call them back. He needed coffee and a cold shower first—and not in that order.

The coffee came with a surprise visit from his landlord. Kurt at his door never meant anything good, and this was no exception.

"You gotta help me, Donovan." Kurt pushed past J.D. and poured himself a cup of J.D.'s coffee. "I got a foreclosure notice from the bank."

"What do you want me to do?"

"Another one of those lump-sum checks would be good."

J.D. shook his head. "I don't have that kind of cash."

"Look, man, anything you could give me would really help out."

"Kurt, man, we've had this conversation before. What about your other three tenants?"

"Actually, it's only two now. The Firestones moved to Florida at Christmas." Kurt shifted his feet. "You know, if the bank forecloses, we're all screwed."

J.D. grabbed his checkbook and calculator from the drawer. "I'll give you something, but it's not going to be much. That lump sum you got was a one-time deal."

"Understood. Thanks, man." Kurt leaned over the table, picked up a brochure from the box, and skimmed it while J.D. crunched numbers. "You think these guys could help me out?"

J.D. looked up. "What guys?"

Kurt waved the brochure.

J.D. grabbed it out of his hand. "You can't afford them."

"Aren't these the guys that bailed you out?"

"Yeah, but look around. I'm not exactly living large."

"I don't want to live large. I just want to keep what I got." Kurt pulled a chair close to J.D. and dropped into it. "C'mon, man, couldn't you put in a word?"

J.D. shook his head.

Kurt peered back in the box and pulled out a business card. "Jason 'J.D.' Donovan, Sales." He looked at J.D. with his eyebrow raised.

J.D. grabbed the card. "I couldn't make my payments. Now I'm an indentured servant. I'm trying to spare you that same fate."

"You were desperate when you signed with them?"

J.D. nodded.

"I'm desperate now. I'm asking for a lifeline." Kurt turned on the puppy dog eyes.

J.D. kept silent. Kurt's naked begging made him twitch. He took a moment to size up his landlord, who was not the shrewdest of businessmen. More butter knife than steak knife. His supposedly shrewd investments were cement shoes drowning him in debt. But it wasn't his fault that his tenants kept moving away or that there weren't enough people left around here to replace them.

Kurt leaned back in his chair. "Look, you've done your due diligence. You warned me, and I didn't listen. Now sign me up."

Should J.D. tell him? Would it make a difference? Kurt seemed so focused on the immediate gain that J.D. doubted he'd give a damn about the long-term consequences.

J.D. grabbed the enrollment form from the box and a pen from the drawer. "Are you sure? These guys are no joke."

Kurt answered without hesitation. "I'm sure. Just tell me where to sign."

Minutes later, J.D.'s first sale was complete.

11.

The next night, J.D. was back on his stool at the bar, trying to drown his guilt in cheap beer. How many people had he killed now? Three for sure, plus whoever Kurt offered up as sacrifices. But that wasn't the worst of it.

The worst of it was that he'd put his own kid in danger. Over what? Bills? Money? He was risking his son's life—his *son*, the one and only priceless thing that he had. What the hell gave him the right to do *that*? A parent's job is to protect their kid, not put them on the chopping block. But that's exactly what he'd done.

J.D. slammed his beer bottle on the bar. It was up to him to fix it. How, he had no idea.

But he needed to find a way out of this whole Deces mess.

Halfway through his third beer, J.D. felt the itchiness of someone staring at him. He turned around and found Gray standing a few feet back, a nervous expression on his face.

He raised his bottle. "Gray! Pull up a stool. I'm buying. Whatever you want, it's on me."

Gray accepted with a nod. He hauled himself onto the stool on J.D.'s right, but said nothing and avoided eye contact.

J.D. waved for the bartender, some young gun that he'd never seen before. He studied Gray with concern. "You okay, buddy?"

Gray, eyes focused on the bar, nodded.

"You sure? You're usually much better at conversating. Gift of the gab. That's you."

Gray shrugged.

The bartender—with his tight t-shirt, muscled physique, and none of Lisa's ease—finally moseyed down to their end of the bar. J.D. ordered two beers. He watched the newbie chase his tail looking for them. Finally, J.D. hauled himself up, leaned over, and pointed out the bottles he wanted. He dropped back onto his seat. "Hard to find good help these days, eh, Gray?"

Gray didn't touch the bottle placed in front of him. He didn't even look at it.

J.D. swung around to face him, eager to hone in on someone else's problems, to push his own away for even a moment. "All right. No joke. Something's going on with you. What gives?"

Gray glanced at J.D., but didn't hold eye contact. Was he scared? Nervous? Embarrassed? The only thing J.D. was sure of was that Gray was sober. For the first time in memory, he emitted no alcohol fumes. A dry Gray was the sign of something momentous.

"C'mon, man, talk to me. Maybe I can help. Even if I can't, just talking will help you feel better. Or so I've heard."

Gray reached for his beer bottle, his hand moving in slow motion. Instead of drinking it, he picked at the label. When he spoke, his voice was quiet, shaky. "Heard you got a job."

J.D. exhaled sharply. "Where did you hear that?"

"Around."

"Kurt."

Gray shrugged.

J.D. took a long swig of beer. No point in denying anything now. "Yeah, I got a job."

"Helping people with money problems?"

Shit. "Sort of. More like, selling people false hope. Why?"

Gray's focus stayed on his beer bottle. Bit by bit, he tore off the label, dropping the pieces in a neat pile on his napkin. "I could use some hope, even if it is the false kind. Think you could sell me some?"

Kurt had said pretty much the same thing. Had J.D. been that desperate, too? Was that why he'd signed with Deces? It had only been a few months, but it felt like decades. Like a bad dream that faded from memory until only a vague outline remained.

J.D. sighed. This was Kurt all over again. Kurt hadn't listened, but maybe J.D. could get through too Gray, spare Gray the same agony that J.D. and Cora Simmons had experienced. He set down his beer. "I could. But you should know: the price is high. As much as these folks say they're flexible, they're not. And they're not forgiving. They will hunt you down and every single person you love, every person you ever cared the smallest fig for."

Movement in the Budweiser mirror behind the bar caught J.D.'s eye. Someone tall and pale flickered along the wall by the pool table. J.D. blinked. Deces? First the hockey game. Then his dream. Now the bar. Either Deces was stalking him, or J.D. was hallucinating. Neither option was good.

If Gray noticed any change in J.D.'s demeanor, he didn't let on. "I've got nowhere else to go, nothing and no one left to lose. I either sign my life away to you or line up for a cot at the church shelter."

The weight of resignation settled on J.D. "Okay. I don't have any of the paperwork with me now. Meet me back here tomorrow night, and I'll walk you through everything."

Gray sagged, his face the picture of relief. "Thanks, man." Then he left, his beer bottle naked but otherwise untouched.

Kurt and Gray were only the beginning. Each night at the bar, someone else found J.D. and begged him to sign them up. He tried his best to warn away each and every one, but they were all as determined as J.D.'s first two customers.

Friday night, right about the time the puck dropped in the Red Wings game, Carl—one of Charlie Simmons's pool buddies—sidled up to J.D.

Roy waved his hand. "You want to do business, fine, but not here. Go find a table."

"Fair enough." J.D. led Carl to a table in the far corner. "What can I do for you, Carl?"

The rest of the conversation followed the usual pattern: Carl was desperate. He'd heard J.D. had a way out, damn the consequences.

J.D. softened his manner and his voice. "Carl, you remember what happened to Charlie?"

Carl nodded.

"I can't prove it, but I think these Final Solution folks did that to him."

With a tsk, Carl dismissed J.D.'s claim. "What happened to Charlie was a tragedy, J.D., but it wasn't murder. It was one of those weird freaks of medicine. Even the doctors said so."

Turning into a human raisin was more than just a "weird freak of medicine," but that debate was better left for another time. "Well, regardless, this firm hurts people—and I don't want anything to happen to you or your loved ones."

"I don't got any loved ones, J.D. My wife left. My kids aren't talking to me. The only people I hear from are the collection agencies. I've got nothing left to lose."

J.D. sighed. He knew the tune Carl was singing. He'd been whistling it himself when all this shit started. "I get it. I just want you to know what you're getting into."

"Okay."

J.D. walked Carl through the paperwork. By the end of the first period of the hockey game, J.D. had made yet another sale.

Within a week, J.D. had signed up eight people. Success had never felt so bad. He showered twice a day and still never felt clean. His gut ached on the regular, in a way that no fancy probiotics or antacids were able to help. But then he'd see Nick, or hear his son's voice on the phone, and he knew he'd have to keep going. Every sale, every sacrifice, bought Nick time.

And everywhere J.D. looked, there was Deces—a fleeting glimpse in a window, a flicker behind a curtain, a smudge that J.D. could never quite wipe off his glasses, a thirst that all the beers at Benji's couldn't quench.

"You keep this up, you're gonna be our next Gray," Roy half-joked as he slid J.D. his third beer of the night. "Which is too bad. I'd always figured you for the sober sort."

J.D. stared at his own reflection in the Budweiser mirror. "People change."

"Only if they absolutely have to. And even then, not very often."

"Consider me the exception that proves the rule." J.D. chugged his drink, slamming the bottle down when he was done.

In the mirror, Deces smiled.

12.

The full moon that month was obscured by clouds, but J.D. knew that wouldn't stop Deces from making his collection. Nothing stopped him. So J.D. sat at his kitchen table in the dark, holding the envelope of money he knew Deces would not accept, waiting for inevitable knock on the door.

At sunrise, with pink light streaming through the window, J.D. still sat at the table, his chin on his chest, envelope on the floor where his sleeping hand had dropped it. He blinked awake and looked around in confusion. Deces never missed a collection. Why had he missed this one?

J.D. stood, groaning at the achy stiffness in his joints. He stretched the knots out of his shoulders and back. Reaching down to his toes, he noticed a manila envelope on the floor, one corner still under the door. It had no stamp, no return address, just *Mr. J. Donovan* written across it in fancy script.

J.D.'s heart pounded. Handwriting that old-fashioned could only belong to Deces. He slid out the single sheet of paper inside. The page was as fancy and old-fashioned as the writing: a sheet of parchment, words written in heavy dark ink like from a fountain pen.

> *Dear Mr. Donovan,*
>
> *Congratulations on becoming a top seller for Final Solution Financial Services. You have exceeded our wildest expectations. Because of your unprecedented success, your payment for this month has been forgiven.*
>
> *We look forward to your continued good work.*
>
> *Sincerely,*
> *Morton Deces*

J.D. found himself sitting on the floor. How was offering people up as sacrifices "good work"? How many people had died because of his "unprecedented success"? How many more needed to die before Deces would set him free?

His stomach tied itself into an intricate knot. Bile gathered in his throat. He had to find a way out. For real, this time.

He searched his paperwork for that PO Box number. Number in hand, he scrawled a note and stuffed it in the Final Solution mailbox.

At midnight, Deces's crisp knock pulled J.D. out of his doze. Dozing in his armchair was the closest thing to sleep he could manage these days. He swung his feet to the ground and shuffled to the door, girding himself with each step for the confrontation that would follow.

J.D. barely had the door open before Deces strode through. He waved J.D.'s note. "You wanted to see me, Mr. Donovan."

J.D. took a deep breath. "I did. I do." He breathed deeply one more time. "I want out."

Deces raised his Spock eyebrow. "Out?"

"Out."

Deces gave him an I-told-you-so smirk. "You wish to be released from your contract?"

J.D. nodded.

Deces motioned to the dining area, and the two men assumed what had become their usual seats. "Perhaps I should explain the consequences before you insist on that option." Deces set his forearms on the table and clasped his hands. "If you were to cancel your agreement with Final Solution, all debts will be returned to you, all help we have given will be rescinded. Your life will be as it was before we met."

"And Gallagher? Charlie? Lisa? What happens to them?"

Deces spread his hands. "Nothing. I cannot resurrect the dead, Mr. Donovan."

J.D. did his best to keep a poker face, but that didn't stop his insides from falling out. His life before he met Deces—unable to pay a single bill, isolated from his son, furnishings listed on Craigslist, collection agencies blowing up his phone, too broke to afford the blue box of mac and cheese. Could J.D. really go back to that? And then there were Gallagher and Charlie and Lisa. If things went back to before, their deaths would have been for nothing. For less than nothing. Could J.D. live with that?

Deces had said that J.D. didn't have the stomach for the sales job. Turns out, he didn't have the stomach for giving it up either. "Let me think on it. I'll have an answer for you on the next full moon."

As had become his habit lately, J.D. sought the answer in the bottom of a beer bottle at the bar. He must have worn his mood like a shield, because for once, no one approached him. Even the newest newbie bartender kept a respectful distance.

Meanwhile, voices jabbered in J.D.'s head. Gallagher, Charlie, Lisa—they all came to visit, with occasional interruptions by Kurt, Gray, and Carl. J.D. put his beer down and covered his ears. That's when he saw Deces in the mirror, wearing a smile that looked more like a sneer.

He turned around. He hadn't hallucinated it. Deces stood a few feet from the pool table. With a smooth wave, he invited J.D. to a nearby table.

J.D. grabbed his beer and accepted the invitation.

"Mr. Donovan, I need a word." He gestured for J.D. to sit.

"I'll stand."

Deces took his seat and crossed his legs. "I have a bit of a dilemma, Mr. Donovan."

J.D. crossed his arms. "I told you. You'll get my answer at the full moon."

"I will, indeed. This is in regard to another matter." Deces paused. "Your name has been given as a proxy for one of our clients."

J.D. swallowed hard. Proxies had very short lives, and he wasn't ready for the end of his just yet. Especially for. . . who? Who the hell had given Deces his name? Kurt? Gray? No wonder Charlie had been so angry.

"However, you are also a very valuable asset to us."

Was that a light at the end of the tunnel?

"So I need to know exactly where your loyalties lie."

J.D. nodded, his brain still trying to untangle the mystery of Deces's words. "I think I need to know a bit more, Mr. Deces."

"Such as?"

"Such as who named me as their proxy."

"Elaine Webster."

J.D's thoughts spun and tumbled. Elaine Webster? His ex-wife Elaine?

That sure explained a lot of other things. Like why she kept harassing J.D. for child support, why she insisted on money instead of accepting the court-approved barter. Why couldn't she just say she was having trouble making ends meet? Not that he would have been any more able to help, but he sure would have been more willing. Not *a lot* more willing, for sure, and he would have given her a hard time, given back more than a little of what she'd given him lately. But he would have done something—for Nick's sake, if nothing else.

J.D. took a swig of beer. "So, what are my options?"

Deces gave him that slippery smile again. "I am glad you asked. As you know, proxies pay a particular price, one we at Final Solution would rather not extract from you given your record of service. So, in light of your role in sales—specifically, your record as one of our top sellers—we are prepared to make you a one-time offer."

Deces paused, clearly more for dramatic effect than anything else.

"Mr. Donovan, if you take on Ms. Webster's debt as your own, we will release her from her contract and you from your obligation as her proxy. In return, we would expect you to meet a certain sales quota each month."

J.D. took a deep breath. "What would that quota be?"

"We would expect you to match the number of sales you made last month, every month."

"For how many months?"

"Until we tell you that all debts—yours and Ms. Webster's—have been settled."

"That could be forever!" J.D.'s beer bottle slammed onto the table.

Deces held up a cautioning hand. "There is no need for melodrama, Mr. Donovan."

"But you're saying it could be six months or the rest of my life—and you're not going to tell me which one?"

Deces nodded.

So the light at the end of the tunnel was really an oncoming train. "I need time to think it over," J.D. told him.

"That is a fair request. You have twenty-four hours. I will meet you tomorrow night at your apartment. Sleep well, Mr. Donovan."

J.D. watched Deces stroll out of the bar. He trudged out a few minutes later, his heart doing somersaults in his chest. Once outside he pulled his phone out of his pocket and dialed Elaine's number.

13.

J.D. climbed the stairs to Elaine's townhouse, the black-eyed Susans at the base of the steps staring at him in judgement. He should have insisted on meeting at a neutral location. But as always when it came to Elaine—to pretty much everything, he'd come to realize—he found it easier to go along then to stand up. That's pretty much how he ended up in this mess in the first place: going along with Deces instead of taking a stand. Sure, he'd tried to defend himself—against Elaine and against Deces—but those stands had been as wobbly as a toddler learning to walk. Well, it was put up or shut up time—and J.D. didn't have any confidence in either option.

Elaine swung open the door as J.D. raised his hand to knock. The put-together woman in the pantsuit from the hockey game was gone. In her place was a woman that J.D. didn't recognize—pale, disheveled, unkempt. Nick's birth almost eighteen years ago had been difficult, and Elaine had experienced such severe complications that she'd almost died. Even under those dire circumstances, she looked better than she did now.

She waved J.D. in without saying a word.

J.D. followed her to the dining nook, his mind filling with questions as they moved. Why was everything so dirty? He could plant seeds in the thick dust on the credenza. What happened to the immaculate housekeeper he'd once lived with? And Elaine's photo collection, where was that? Her nature photography had taken pride of place on their walls, once upon a time. There wasn't a single bird or butterfly or flower to be seen. In fact, her walls seemed unusually bare.

Once in the nook, Elaine sat at the table and wrapped her hands around an oversized coffee mug. J.D. wanted to sit next to her, take her hand, offer comfort. Instead, he took the seat opposite. Between them sat a very familiar-looking mountain of envelopes. They sat in silence, the air filling with uncertainty.

J.D. finally broke the silence, making an effort to keep his voice calm and neutral. He waved at the pile of bills. "Why didn't you tell me things were this bad?"

Something like life or anger flickered in Elaine's eyes and then disappeared. "I hounded you for child support."

"But you never said that you *needed* it, that you were having trouble making ends meet. I'm not saying I could have paid, but I would have done *something*."

"So do something now."

J.D. closed his eyes and sighed. "I'm trying. What happened to that big check you called me about?"

"It helped. It did. It just . . . wasn't enough."

"Jesus, Elaine, how far under are you?"

That flicker of steel showed again. "You don't get to know that."

"I'm not asking out of idle curiosity." J.D. put his hands on the table and pushed himself up. "I need a cup of coffee." He found Elaine's coffee machine, popped in a pod, and waited. While the machine whirred, he surveyed the clutter hanging on the refrigerator. Business cards, take-out menus, school announcements, a couple of photos of Nick, and—much to J.D.'s surprise—a photo of him and Elaine in happier days. He picked up the photo and studied it. It wasn't a newlywed photo. It was from much later, a trip to Mackinac Island. Nick must have been about eight or nine. He'd gone somewhere with friends, and J.D. and Elaine took advantage. Those really had been the good old days.

The coffee mug full, J.D. rehung the photo and resumed his place at the dining table. "So how did you hook up with Final Solution?"

Elaine pulled her sweater tighter around herself. "How'd you know about that? It's supposed to be confidential."

"Then you shouldn't have named me as your proxy."

Elaine sighed. Her story was much like J.D.'s—Deces had shown up at her door, promised an end to all her troubles, and left with a signed contract.

"You know, I work for them now. For Final Solution. For Deces."

Elaine's eyes widened.

"I've learned things about them, about how they work. They're dangerous, Elaine." He told her what he knew—about Gallagher and Charlie and Lisa, about being coerced into selling for them, and about the latest deal that Deces had offered him.

Elaine took a deep breath. J.D could see her mulling over his story. When she spoke, she did so tentatively. "So . . . you either take on my debt or Deces takes your life?"

J.D. nodded.

Her fire came back again, and this time it stayed. "That's not fair. You shouldn't die because I can't pay my bills. Besides, Nick needs you. I—"

J.D. had no difficulty filling in the blank, though he doubted she was right. "I agree it's unfair, but those are the only choices I have. Unless you see another way?"

Elaine shook her head. "If I could only take back your name."

"You mean as a proxy? Who would you be sentencing to death then? Your mother? Your neighbor? Suzy from third grade?"

Her mug hit the table with a thud. "Better one of them than the father of my child."

"Really, Elaine? Even your Mom? You don't mean that."

She gave him a steely gaze that reminded him just how strong she was. "She's almost 90 years old. She's lived her life. Hell, so have you, but Nick hasn't, and he deserves to have his dad."

"That wasn't the tune you were singing a few months ago."

"Really, J.D.? That's where you want to go?"

J.D. shook his head. "Sorry. I couldn't help it. But how could you knowingly sentence someone else to death? How would you make a choice like that?"

Elaine breathed deep. "Some people deserve death. Murders. Pedophiles—"

"But we're not talking about those kinds of people. We're talking about everyday people, people like you and me, people we *know*. Where do you draw the line? How do you decide who lives and who dies?"

Elaine squared her shoulders. She punctuated every word with a finger tap on the table. "You do what you have to do to save your child."

"I'm not arguing that." J.D. sat back in his chair. "Look, we both attended Sunday school. We both had to memorize the Ten Commandments. Remember 'Thou shalt not kill'? 'Thou shalt not steal'? What gives you or me or any other ordinary Joe the right to break those commandments, to steal another person's life, to kill them?"

Elaine said nothing, so J.D. continued. "And if you did break those commandments, could you live with yourself? Could you really, truly, honestly look yourself in the mirror ever again? Because I sure as hell can't."

Elaine's shoulders fell, like a balloon deflating. "You're right."

"So what do we do?"

"Call the police."

J.D. shook his head. "I thought of that already. It wouldn't work."

They turned over the problem until they'd drained their coffee mugs and emptied a bottle of wine. J.D. was cracking open another bottle when the front door opened and slammed shut.

"MOM! I'm home!" Nick's voice carried throughout the house.

J.D. and Elaine shared a look. What would the boy think, seeing his parents half in their cups at the dining table?

Without breaking eye contact, Elaine answered. "In here!"

Nick clomped in, dropping his backpack with a *thud* when he saw J.D. "Dad? What are you doing here?

Elaine studied the bottom of her wineglass.

J.D. waved at a chair. "Have a seat, son."

"Are you two getting back to together or something?"

"No, nothing like that."

"Dad, are you moving away? Mom, are we?"

J.D. and Elaine shook their heads almost in unison.

J.D. pushed away his wineglass and folded his hands on the table. "Nick, you remember when you told me something was going on with your mom?"

Elaine's head shot up. She looked quickly from Nick to J.D. and back at Nick again.

Nick didn't seem to notice. His attention was all on J.D. "Yeah. You told me that I was wrong."

"Well, I was the one who was wrong. Your mom, she made a bad deal." J.D. took a deep breath. "And I made an even worse one." He summarized the situation, watching Nick show growing alarm with each sentence. By the time he finished, all color had left his son's face.

"What are you going to do?"

"I don't know."

Nick turned to his mother. "Why didn't you tell me? I could have gotten a job." His face brightened. "I'll get a job now. With two incomes—"

"No." Elaine's tone brooked no argument. "Your job is hockey and school. You need a scholarship to pay for college. Hockey and good grades are your only chances."

Nick looked at J.D., who responded, "Your mom's right."

Nick's expression turned to utter helplessness. J.D. knew the feeling. By the time he left an hour later, he still had no idea what he was going to do. He only knew that he couldn't let Nick down.

14.

Deces arrived just after sunset, as the moon started its ascent in the night sky. As usual, he strode into J.D.'s flat as if it were his own and assumed his place at the table. He leaned back, lifted his right foot onto his knee, and drummed his fingers on the table. "Well, Mr. Donovan, have you made your decision?"

J.D. breathed deeply, searching for an escape route. An idea took shape. He met Deces's gaze. "I'd like to make a counteroffer."

Deces raised his eyebrow. "Go on."

J.D. took another deep breath. "Instead of taking my life as a proxy for Elaine's debt, take Elaine's life instead."

Deces's fingers froze and despite himself, J.D.'s heart lifted. "That is a novel idea. What would the rewards of that be?"

"I would get custody of my son, for one. And the money I'd get from selling her house and belongings would settle her debt with you."

"Hmmmm." Deces stood and paced the kitchenette. "You would continue your role as a sales associate in regard to your own debt?"

A heaviness formed in J.D.'s gut. He wanted out of that, too. But what would a no cost him? Deces had already threatened Nick, and more than once. This time, for a change, J.D. was determined to save his family. He swallowed hard. "Yes."

Deces paced another five—six—laps. J.D. monitored every elegant step. Finally, Deces stopped, turned on his heel, and offered J.D. his hand. "You have a deal, Mr. Donovan."

J.D. sighed. He was halfway there. "So, how does it work?"

"You give me the name. I perform a ceremony—"

"No." J.D. planted his feet and crossed his arms. "If I'm going to be responsible for taking a life, then I want—I need—to actually do the deed. For once in my life, I need to take responsibility and DO a damn thing instead of letting life roll over me and just accepting the consequences. I hate it, it's ugly, but this mess is all my fault so I'll do it."

Deces eyed J.D., studying him as if he were a fine cut of beef. He lifted his briefcase onto the table. "If you insist."

From the case, he produced a thick black candle, a fireplace match, a sheet of paper, and a fancy pen. With meticulous penmanship, he printed a long series of words. He slid the pen into his jacket pocket and pushed the rest of the items across the table.

J.D. picked up the paper. "What do I do?"

Deces explained in a tone usually reserved for kindergarteners. "You light the candle with that match. You read the words on the paper, then you say the name."

Not the answer J.D. had expected, but far easier than what he'd imagined. He read over the page. He didn't recognize the language, but the syllables seemed simple enough. He mouthed the words as he read them a second and third time.

J.D. closed his eyes and inhaled deeply.

He straightened his posture, struck the match, and touched it to the candle's wick. Once the flame caught, J.D. sounded out the words he'd practiced. Then he slowly pronounced the name, "Morton Deces."

Deces smiled his Cheshire cat grin. He clapped his hands. "Bravo! I'm afraid, though, that's not how it—"

Deces blinked. He seemed pinched. He struggled for breath and grabbed his middle. He bent in half, gasping for air. His body trembled and convulsed. In the blink of an eye and a puff of smoke, Deces disappeared.

J.D. stared at the empty chair. It took a few seconds for him to remember to breathe. He blew out the candle and collapsed into the nearest seat. "It seems, Mr. Deces, that's exactly how it works."

ACKNOWLEDGEMENTS

This story was born in the NYC Midnight 2017 Short Story Challenge. When I received my prompt—horror/door-to-door sales/an unemployed 40-year-old man—I literally danced around my living room chanting "I get to write a Stephen King story!" I've been reading Stephen King books since elementary school, and all those scares finally paid off. Thank you, Mr. King!

It's taken me five years to expand that original 2,000 word story into a novella that I'm happy with, and I have many people to thank for helping me along the way: Julie Hutchings, editor extraordinaire, whose feedback helped me tighten the screws on J.D.; Fantasy & Coffee Design, who created the cover of my dreams; the collection of friends and colleagues who voted on the back cover blurb; and last, but not least, the critique partners and beta readers who helped me patch the plotholes and polish the prose: Debbie Klein, Helene Dunne, Mars D. Gill, Nicole Fruit, Pam Larson, and Chris Schmuker.

ABOUT THE AUTHOR

Ilene Goldman is a short story author and novelist. Her work has appeared in the anthologies *A Wink and a Smile* (Smoking Pen Press, 2018) and *ProleSCARYet* (Rad Flesh Press, 2021). She lives and works in northern Illinois, where she is closely supervised by her two canine editorial assistants. You can find her on Twitter @ilenegold, Instagram @ilenegoldwrites, and the World Wide Web at www.ilenegoldman.com.